Toot & Puddle
The Great
Cheese Chase

Based on the teleplay by Stu Krieger
Adapted by Laura F. Marsh

NATIONAL GEOGRAPHIC
Washington, D.C.

To Lucas and Laurel -

whose mom gave these piggies a whole new life!

Text copyright © 2008 National Geographic Society

Illustrations copyright © 2008 NGE, Inc.

Compilation copyright © 2008 NGS

Based on the television show Toot & Puddle

Characters based on the original series created by Holly Hobbie.

A production of Mercury Filmworks (East) in association with National Geographic Kids Entertainment.

Published by arrangement with NGE.

Founded in 1888, the National Geographic Society is one of the largest nonprofit scientific and educational organizations
in the world. It reaches more than 285 million people worldwide each month through its official journal, NATIONAL GEOGRAPHIC, and its four other
magazines; the National Geographic Channel; television documentaries; radio programs; films; books;
videos and DVDs; maps; and interactive media. National Geographic has funded more than 8,000 scientific research projects
and supports an education program combating geographic illiteracy.

For more information, please call
1-800-NGS LINE (647-5463) or write to the following address:
NATIONAL GEOGRAPHIC SOCIETY
1145 17th Street N.W., Washington, D.C. 20036-4688 U.S.A.

Visit us online at www.nationalgeographic.com/books
Librarians and teachers, visit us at www.ngchildrensbooks.org

For information about special discounts for bulk purchases, please contact
National Geographic Books Special Sales: ngspecsales@ngs.org.

For rights or permissions inquiries, please contact
National Geographic Books Subsidiary Rights: ngbookrights@ngs.org.

Library of Congress Cataloging-in-Publication Data available from the publisher on request.
Trade Paperback ISBN 978-1-4263-0223-7
Reinforced Library Edition ISBN 978-1-4263-0371-5

Printed in USA

"I can't wait for our trip!" Toot told Puddle and Tulip as they ate breakfast in the kitchen of their cottage.

Toot was listing all of the things he wanted to do in Paris. "We can go to the Eiffel Tower, the amazing museums—"

"And eat the delicious cheese!" interrupted Puddle.

"I know, I know. That's all you've talked about!" Toot laughed.

"Once we get to France, can we go straight to Le Chateau du Fromage?" said Puddle.

"What's that?" Tulip asked.

"It's the best cheese shop in Paris," said Puddle dreamily. "It means the castle of cheese."

As their plane landed in Paris, Toot and Puddle heard a voice come over the loudspeaker.

"Welcome to France, where the mademoiselles do the can-can dance! From the River Seine to the Eiffel Tower, we hope you enjoy each and every hour."

As soon as they arrived,
Puddle bought Toot a French
hat, called a beret, and they
began sightseeing at once.

They climbed every step of
the Eiffel Tower.

They went to the Louvre, the most famous museum in France. There they saw the Mona Lisa, one of the most famous paintings in France.

"What do you think she's smiling about?" Toot asked.

"She's probably eaten some cheese from Le Chateau du Fromage!" said Puddle.

"Okay, I get the hint," Toot said. "We need to find the cheese shop."

At the outdoor market, Toot looked at his map. "It should be this way," he said. But Puddle had wandered off to a nearby fruit stand.

"You must have a taste," the fruit vendor said. "Each bite is sure to delight."

"Sold!" said Toot.

There sure was a lot to see—and eat—in Paris.

Some of the food was even fun to play with.

After sampling many different kinds of French cuisine, Puddle asked hopefully, "To the cheese shop?"

"What's the rush, Puds?" said Toot. "We'll get there. You know what I always say: the more places you go, the more things you know!"

Toot and Puddle found a bakery selling crepes.
"Wow, they look delicious!" Puddle exclaimed.
"What are they?" asked Toot.

"It's a pancake, it's a pancake, called a crepe! Called a crepe!
It's sweet and quite delicious, healthy and nutritious.
Fun to make! Fun to make!"
a nearby street musician sang.

On their way out of the bakery, Puddle stopped to talk to the musician.

"Say, do you know where Le Chateau du Fromage is?" Puddle asked the musician.

"Of course," he answered. "Go to the end of the block and turn left."

"We're almost there," said Toot.

"Let's run for it!" Puddle cried.

Rounding the corner, Puddle spied what they'd been searching for. The storefront window of Le Chateau du Fromage was truly amazing.

The shop owner offered Toot
and Puddle a taste. "If I eat
it all myself, it's very bad for
business," he explained.

"I'm afraid we've had too
many treats today," said Toot,
shaking his head sadly and
patting his very full belly.
Puddle's belly was full, too.

"How about taking a gift box
home instead?" the shop owner
suggested.

Toot and Puddle agreed that
was a great idea.

Back home at Woodcock Pocket,
Tulip was happy to see her
friends again. And Toot and
Puddle were glad to be home.

"Yummy," said Tulip with a mouth full of cheese. "Don't you want some?"

"Merci, but non," Puddle replied.

"That means, 'thank you, but no' in French," explained Toot.

"Don't worry," Toot answered. "We'll enjoy the cheese later."

"Much later," Puddle said, patting his tummy with a chuckle.